Hello, Family Members,

Learning to read is one of the most important accomplishments of early childhood. **Hello Reader!** books are designed to help children become skilled readers who like to read. Beginning readers learn to read by remembering frequently used words like "the," "is," and "and"; by using phonics skills to decode new words; and by interpreting picture and text clues. These books provide both the stories children enjoy and the structure they need to read fluently and independently. Here are suggestions for helping your child *before*, *during*, and *after* reading:

Before

- Look at the cover and pictures and have your child predict what the story is about.
- Read the story to your child.
- Encourage your child to chime in with familiar words and phrases.
- Echo read with your child by reading a line first and having your child read it after you do.

During

- Have your child think about a word he or she does not recognize right away. Provide hints such as "Let's see if we know the sounds" and "Have we read other words like this one?"
- Encourage your child to use phonics skills to sound out new words.
- Provide the word for your child when more assistance is needed so that he or she does not struggle and the experience of reading with you is a positive one.
- Encourage your child to have fun by reading with a lot of expression . . . like an actor!

After

- Have your child keep lists of interesting and favorite words.
- Encourage your child to read the books over and over again. Have him or her read to brothers, sisters, grandparents, and even teddy bears. Repeated readings develop confidence in young readers.
- Talk about the stories. Ask and answer questions. Share ideas about the funniest and most interesting characters and events in the stories.

I do hope that you and your child enjoy this book.

— Francie Alexander
Chief Education Officer,
Scholastic's Learning Ventures

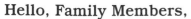

To Dr. Michael Neuwirth and his superb
team at Beth Israel, with many thanks for their
expert knowledge and skill
— R.H.

With gratitude to Mr. Lou Patrei,
the staff, and especially the teachers, past and
present, of the Benton Hall Academy
— J.S.

Go to scholastic.com for web site information on
Scholastic authors and illustrators.

ISBN 0-439-31707-X

Library of Congress Cataloging-in-Publication Data is available.

10 9 8 7 6 5 4 3 2 1   02 03 04 05 06
Printed in the U.S.A.   24
First printing, March 2002

BONES!

All Kinds of Hands,
All Kinds of Feet

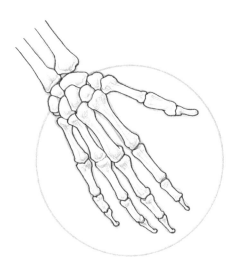

by Rosanna Hansen
Illustrated by Joel Snyder

Hello Reader! Science— Level 3

SCHOLASTIC INC.

New York   Toronto   London   Auckland   Sydney
Mexico City   New Delhi   Hong Kong   Buenos Aires

CHAPTER ONE

Strong Stuff

Your bones are strong.
In fact, they are four times
stronger than concrete!

Bones hold up your body.
Without bones, you couldn't stand up.
Your body would fall down in a heap.
You would look like a big blob of jelly!

Bones come in many shapes and sizes.
The biggest bones are in your legs.
The smallest bones are in your ears.
Your ear bones are about the size of
your little fingernail!

Bones are hard.
They help to protect your soft insides.
The bones in your head make up your *skull*.
Your skull is like a helmet.
It protects your brain.
The bones in your chest are called *ribs*.
The ribs are like a cage.
They protect your lungs and heart.
Together, all your bones make up your *skeleton*.

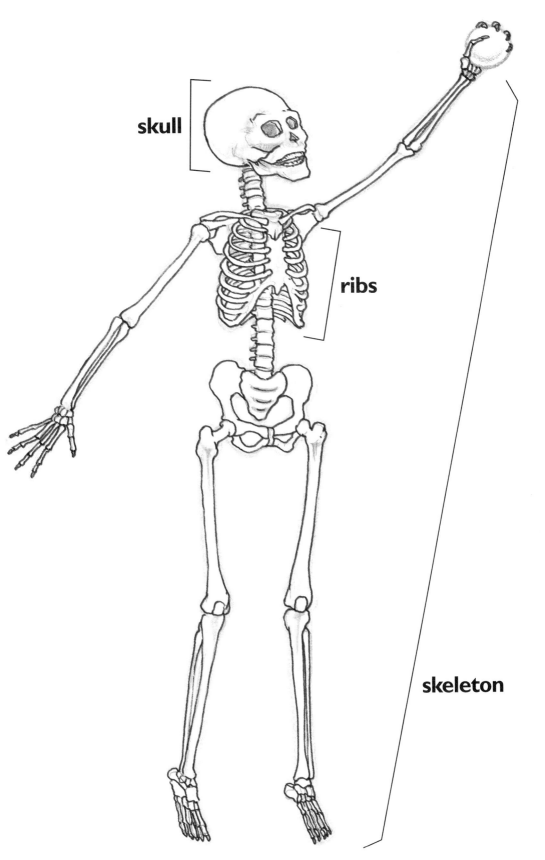

skull

ribs

skeleton

Try moving your arm up and down.
Did you use your elbow?
Your elbow helps your arm bones move.
It is called a *joint*.
Joints are the places where your bones
are joined together.
Your joints help you move and bend.

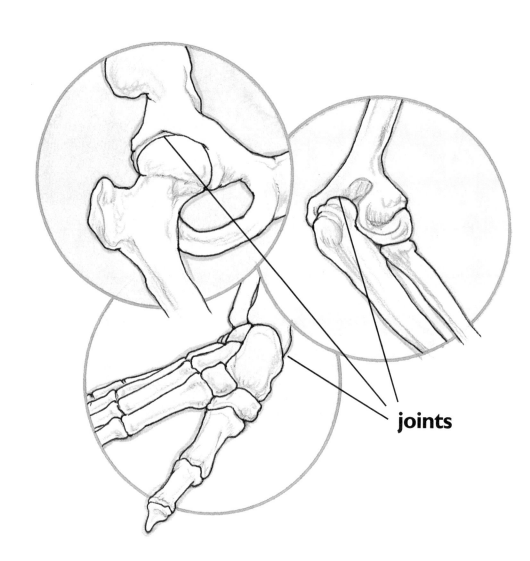

joints

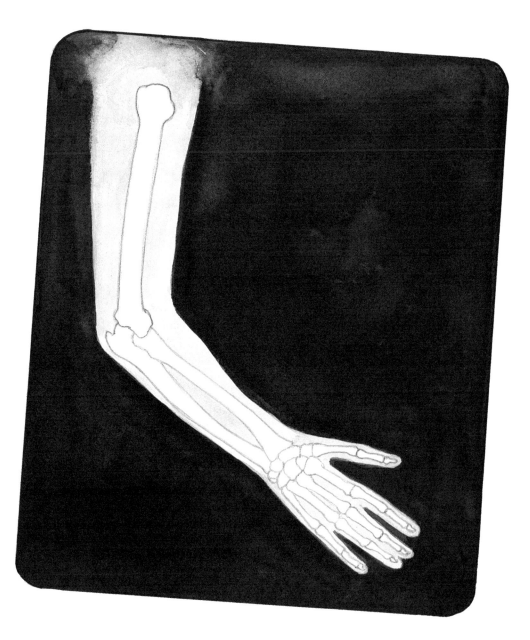

X rays are special pictures of your bones.
This is how an X ray looks.
Your doctor may take an X ray to see
how your bones are growing.

As you grow, your bones keep
getting bigger and harder.
That's why you get taller every year.
As your bones grow, some of them
actually grow together to make
one bigger bone.
By the time you are about 20 years old,
your bones will stop growing
and changing.
You will be fully grown,
with 206 adult bones in your body.

CHAPTER TWO

Your Hands and Feet

Your hands are amazing.
They can throw a ball,
paint a picture, pick up a pin,
scratch an itch, and do
hundreds of other jobs.

3 BALLS / $1

Inside each of your hands are
19 little bones.
No wonder your hands can
do so many different things.
Humans have two hands.
Each hand has four fingers and a thumb.
The thumb is a special part of your hand.
It helps you hold things.
Try to button a button
without using your
thumb.
Can you do it?
Now button a button
using your thumb
and fingers.
Which way
is easier?

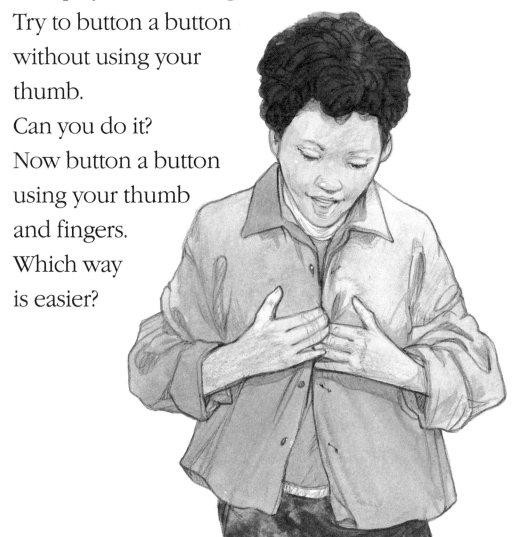

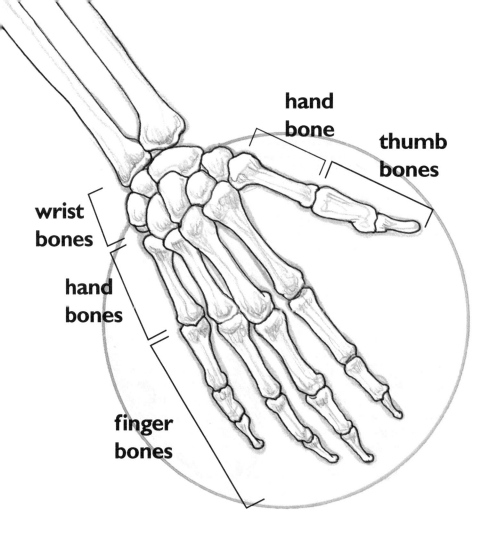

hand
bone

thumb
bones

wrist
bones

hand
bones

finger
bones

Next, bend and wiggle your fingers.
See how easily they move?
Try counting the bones in the fingers
and thumb of one hand.
How many did you count?
If you counted 14, you are right!
All these bones help your fingers
and thumb move freely.

Now wiggle your wrist.
Feel how easily it moves?
There are eight
small bones in
your wrist.
They help your
wrist move up,
down, and sideways.

Next, look at your feet.
In each foot, you have seven anklebones,
five foot bones, and 14 toe bones.

See how short your toes are?
Overall, they are shorter and fatter
than your fingers.
Your toes help you keep your balance.

Feet are strong.
They are so strong that dancers can stand
way up on their toes.

Have you ever seen your footprint on wet sand?
If you have, you know it looks like this:

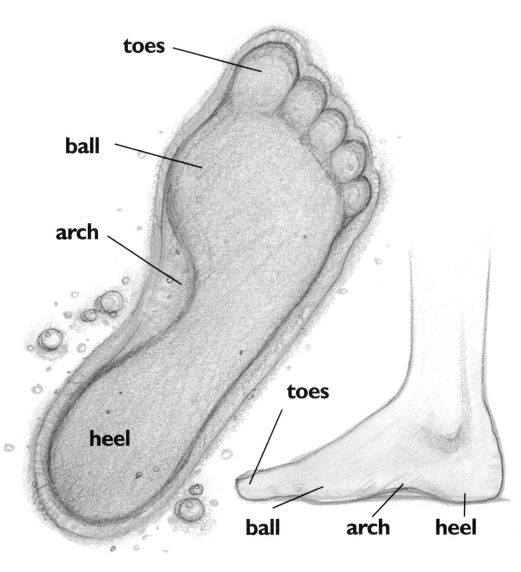

Do you see where the *arch* is in both pictures?
Now look at your own foot.
Can you see your own arch?

The arch acts like a spring.
It helps you leap and jump.
It also makes it easier for you
to walk and run.
A few people do not have
arches in their feet.
We say they have "flat feet."

Your feet are suited to the way you live.
They are good for

walking,

running,

leaping,

jumping,

skipping,

hopping,

and moving lots of other ways.

Your feet help you have fun!

Together, the bones in your hands,
feet, and wrists total nearly half the bones
in your entire body!

CHAPTER THREE

Animal Hands and Feet

Your hands and feet are specially made
for the way you live.
Other creatures have different hands
and feet.
Their hands and feet are suited to
the ways they live.

Going Batty

Bats have wings instead of hands.
Inside their wings are long finger bones.
Flaps of skin stretch between these bones.
On its first finger, the bat has a sharp claw.
This claw helps the bat grab on to its food
or hold tight to a tree.

Water Wings

Penguins have wings, too.
But they can't fly!
Most birds have light bones.
Light bones help birds fly.
Penguins have heavier bones.
They use their wings to swim.
A penguin's foot
has three long toes.
A web of skin
joins the three toes.

Penguins' feet work best in the water.
On land, their feet are slow.
But penguins have a special way to go fast!
First, they lie down on their tummies.
Then they push with their wings and feet.
WHEE!
There they go,
sliding across the ice.

Hanging in There

The sloth has two big claws
on each front leg
and three on each back leg.
Its claws act like huge hooks.
With its claws, the sloth can hang
for hours from a tree.
It can even take a nap upside down!

The sloth's front leg bones are much longer
than its back leg bones. Why?
The sloth uses its front legs to pull itself
along the ground.
The sloth's belly drags on the ground
as it crawls.
No wonder the sloth likes treetops best!
Hanging around is its favorite thing to do.

Dig It!

The bones in the giant armadillo's front legs
are short, but powerful.
The armadillo shovels dirt
with its front legs and thick claws,
digging holes to live in.
It can also tear apart
a termite mound,
looking for a tasty lunch.

Going Ape

The gibbon is a kind of ape.
It likes to swing through the treetops.
Its long thin arm bones help it swing
and swoop.
The gibbon has four long fingers
on each hand.
These fingers work like hooks.
They can snag a branch and hang on tight.

If you were a gibbon, your arms would
reach almost down to your shoes.
You could even tie your shoelaces
while standing up!

The gibbon's feet are different from your feet.
Its big toe works like your thumb—
it can grip and hold on to things!
The gibbon's four other toes are long
and thin, like fingers.
The bones inside its toes are thin and light.
With these special toes, the gibbon can grab
a tree branch or hold some food.
In fact, a gibbon's feet work just like your hands.

Compare the gibbon's hand and
foot to your hand and foot.

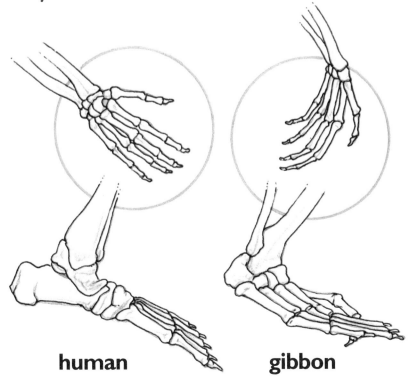

human   **gibbon**

Champion Jumpers

The kangaroo has strong legs
and great big feet.
That's why it can jump so far.
Using its mighty muscles and thighbones,
the kangaroo pushes off.
Up, up, up it goes!
A big kangaroo can soar 25 feet (7.6 meters)
in one jump.

A kangaroo's hands have bones
that are small and thin.
Luckily, the kangaroo doesn't need its hands
for jumping.

Frogs are great jumpers, too.
Like kangaroos, they have
strong leg bones and big feet.
A frog's foot has five toes.
The toes have webbing in between.
When the frog swims,
the toes spread open.
This helps the frog push through water.

One kind of tree frog can even glide
through the air!
First, it spreads its webbed feet out wide.
Then *WHEE!*
Away it goes, gliding
from tree to tree.

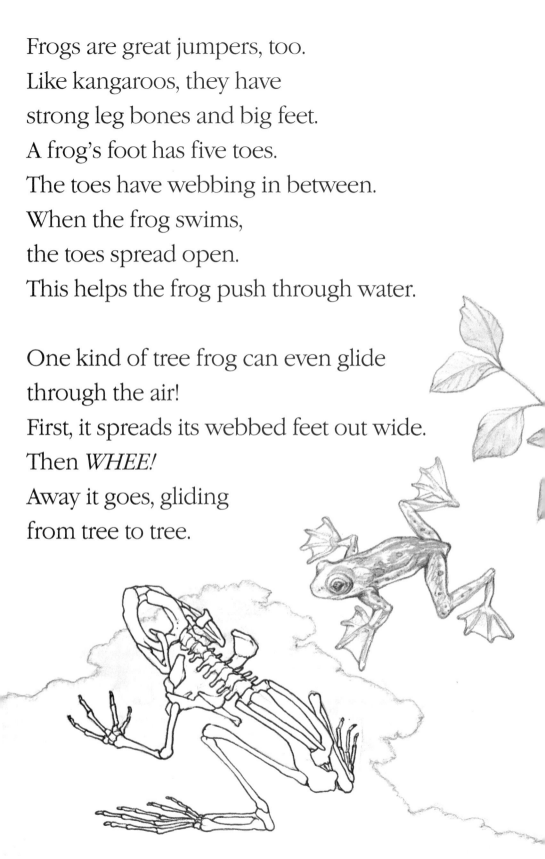

Run Like the Wind

Have you ever seen a horse
racing across a field?
Horses love to run!
And they are built to run like the wind.
They have strong leg bones and feet
that help them run fast.

A horse's foot is really a single toe
that has grown very large.
This large toe ends
in a hoof.
Most of the hoof is like
a big, thick toenail.
It can be cut
without hurting
the horse.
The horse's hard,
thick hooves protect its feet.
So horses can run for miles and
miles and not get hurt.

Flipping Out

Flippers help sea lions swim.
The bones inside the flippers
look like extra-long fingers or toes.
Sea lions paddle with their front flippers.
To steer, they use their back flippers.

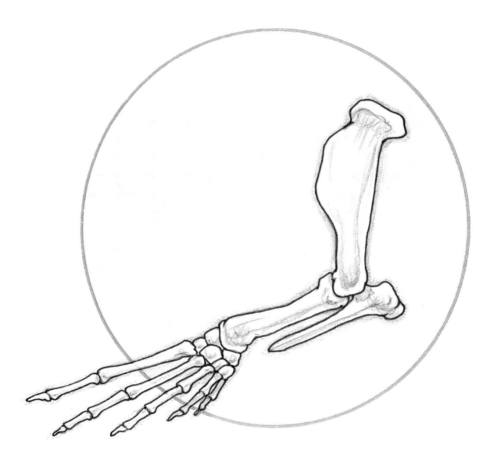

Sea lions can walk with their flippers, too.
You might see them do this at the zoo.
They can even clap their flippers
as a special trick!

Ocean Giant

Blue whales are the largest animals on Earth.
Their skeletons are surprisingly light.
This is because water supports
the whale's weight.

A whale's flippers help it steer
through the water.
The bones in a blue whale's flipper
look like the bones in your hand.
But, a whale has only four fingers,
instead of five.
These fingers are long.

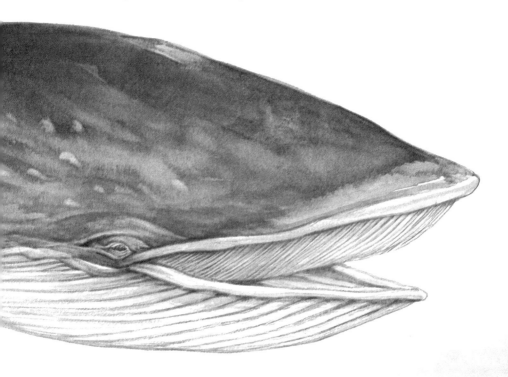

Each of your fingers has three bones.
A whale can have as many as eight bones
in a finger!

Now you know all about the bones
in hands and feet and the jobs they do.
In fact, your hands just turned
the last page of this book.
Good job!